Look What's Under My Bed

Told by Danielle Brenneman
Written by Deborah Wagner-Brenneman
Illustrated by Joe Santoro

Look What's Under My Bed

Published by DAB-A-TAB Books
in partnership with Acorn Book Services

For information call:
or Email: acornbookservices@gmail.com

Designed by Acorn Book Services
Publication Managed by Acorn Book Services
www.acornbooksesrvices.com
acornbookservices@gmail.com
304-995-1295

ISBN-13: 978-0991000302
ISBN-10: 0991000307

Dedicated to my daddy, to whom has taught me the joy of rhyme.
Danielle Brenneman

Dedicated to my beautiful daughters,
Danielle-n-Taryn
and to all the students I have taught and will teach.
For they have touched my life, forever!!
Deborah Wagner-Brenneman
"Mrs. B"

Look what's under my bed.

Take a peek, but don't
bump your head.

As you can see,

there's a dolphin ready to jump.

There is also a camel
with a big funny hump.

If you go farther under my bed
you'll find a yellow tiger
that hasn't been fed.

Oh! Look what is this?
It's a big goldfish.
This big goldfish likes to wish!

Rattle, rattle ...
What's that sound?

A slithering rattlesnake wandering around.

Look at the rabbit
hopping through the air.

He's racing a turtle.
That just isn't fair.

Under my bed,
there is also a shark.
And when I go to bed,
it swims in the dark.

Under my bed

there is a galloping noise.

It seems there's a horse leaping with joy.

Polar Bear, Polar Bear,
get out from there...
Look at the dust
on your pretty white hair.

Boom, boom
with a thrust,

Through my floor
the elephant bust.

Do you hear
that snapping noise?

It is an alligator
eating my toys.

Oh, Mister Lion,
you're so strong & sweet,
but I don't appreciate your roar
when I sleep.

Good-bye, Good night, I must go to sleep!
Get under my bed and not one more peep.
I know under my bed was a blast,
but not every fun thing will forever last.

I left you a blank page.
Now use your own head
to discover some things
that live under your bed.

Photocopy the next page.

Mrs. B's Project Page

Parents and Teachers:

This hands-on book creates character education questions. There are different things occurring that can bring up conversation with children as it is being read or after it has been read.

Examples:

PAGE 8: The camel with a big funny hump can prompt a discussion of how we are all different.

PAGE 9: A tiger that hasn't been fed: Talk about hunger. Talk about nutrition.

PAGE 10: Goldfish making a wish: Talk about wishes, hopes, and dreams.

PAGE 13-14: The turtle and the rabbit racing: Fairness and justice, and difference in how we are all made.

PAGE 20: Elephants busting through: Unforeseen plans in life. Are there ways to prepare? Are there ways to cope?

PAGE 22: Alligator eating my toys: Treating Peoples things the way you want your things to be treated.

PAGE 24: But not every fun thing will last forever. Talk about stages of life and how things in our lives will end but other things will take the place of them.

Made in the USA
Charleston, SC
15 November 2013